Little Funnies is a delightful collection of picture books made to put a giggle into storytime.

There are funny stories about a laughing lobster, a daring mouse, a teeny tiny woman, and lots more colourful characters!

Perfect for sharing, these rib-tickling tales will have your little ones coming back for more!

For Amelia

First published 1995 by Walker Books Ltd
87 Vauxhall Walk, London SE11 5HJ

This edition published 2007

10 9 8 7 6 5 4 3 2 1

This book has been typeset in Plantin.

Printed in China

British Library Cataloguing in Publication Data:
a catalogue record for this book is
available from the British Library.

ISBN 978-1-4063-0791-7

www.walkerbooks.co.uk

One Day in the Jungle

Colin West

WALKER BOOKS
AND SUBSIDIARIES
LONDON • BOSTON • SYDNEY • AUCKLAND

One day in the jungle
there was a little sneeze.

"Bless you, Butterfly!"
said Lizard.

Next day in the jungle
there was a not-quite-so-little sneeze.

“Bless you, Lizard!”
said Parrot.

Next day in the jungle
there was a medium-sized sneeze.

“Bless you, Parrot!”
said Monkey.

Next day in the jungle
there was a big sneeze.

"Bless you, Monkey!"
said Tiger.

Next day in the jungle
there was a very big sneeze.

“Bless you, Tiger!”
said Hippo.

Next day in the jungle
there was an enormous sneeze.

"Bless you, Hippo!"
said Elephant.

Next day in the jungle
there was a **GIGANTIC** sneeze.

ACHOOOOOOO!

“Bless me!” said Elephant.
“I’ve blown away the jungle!”

Little Funnies Joke Time
Which animal is always laughing?
A happy-potamus!